Little Armored One

of the South Plains

A treegryphon Book

By
Elaine Renfro

Illustrated by
Bobbie Dunlap

AuthorHouse™
1663 Liberty Drive
Bloomington, IN 47403
www.authorhouse.com
Phone: 1-800-839-8640

First published by AuthorHouse   12/20/2010

ISBN: 978-1-4520-0962-9

Library of Congress Control Number: 2010917142

Printed in the United States of America

This book is printed on acid-free paper.

authorHOUSE®

To all that binds us together in spirit
For the good of all life on Earth

In memory of my parents

Dedicated to those who walked beside me
throughout my journey of inspiration

Bobbie Dunlap

Alex Garrett

Victoria

Special Friends

Josephine Boutwell

Martha Childs

Vicenta Cloos

Acknowledgements

The author gratefully acknowledges the honorable contributions of Friends of TAMIU Wildlife.

With special thanks to

Dr. Ray M. Keck, III

Dr. Leo Sayavedra

José García

Sue and the late Radcliffe Killam

Richard Gentry

And, of course,

the wildlife that inspired this story

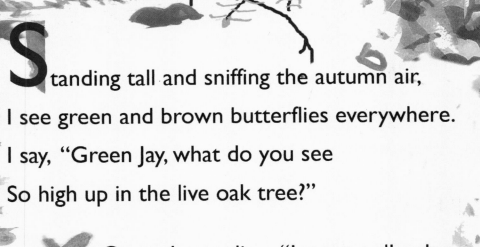

Standing tall and sniffing the autumn air,

I see green and brown butterflies everywhere.

I say, "Green Jay, what do you see

So high up in the live oak tree?"

Green Jay replies, "I see a polka dot symphony.

Among the feather-like leaves of the retama tree,

A hundred green butterflies are winking at me.

What else did I see?

I observed your startled reflex- Jump! Jump! Jump!

...As acorns fell- Pop! Crack! Thump!

You are searching for One Who is Humane, I am told.

To embark on such a journey, you must be very bold.

After you cross the great thicket and woodrat abode,

Talk with the white-tail deer gathered by the road."

I say, "If I am to make it to Smooth Rock today,

I must avoid further delay."

I imagine...Just like Green Jay, I have wings to fly so high and free.
How far I can see!

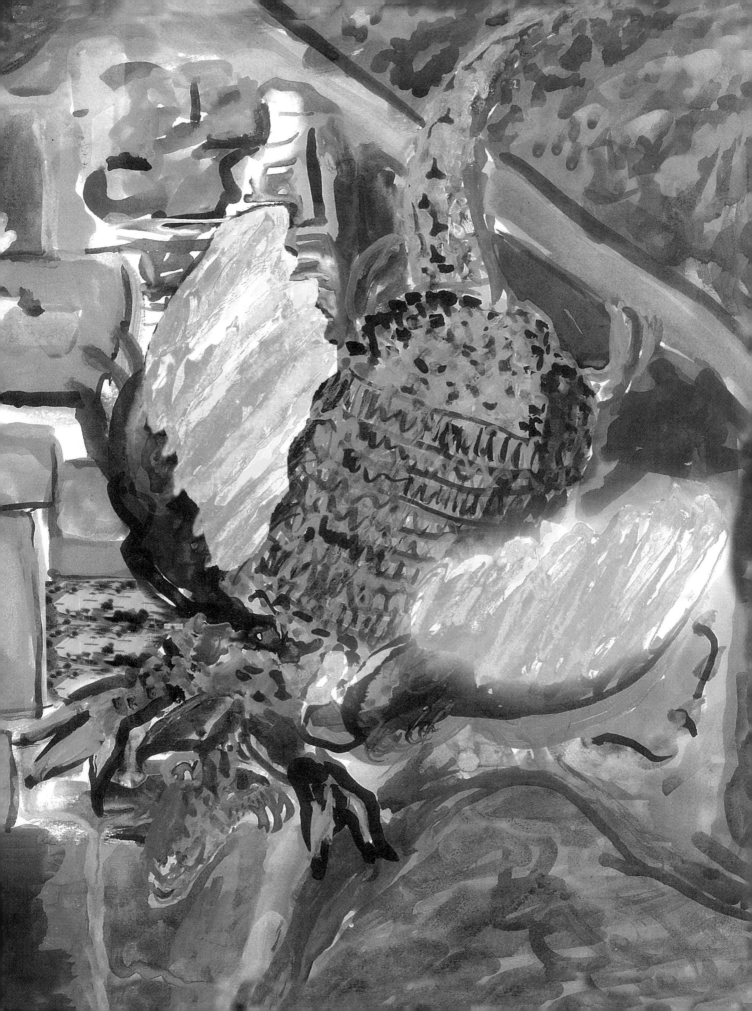

The ancient site of the Tuna Harvest is located nearby,

At the great thicket of prickly pear cacti.

Surrounded by so many faces,

It has long been one of my favorite places.

Yellow flowers, sweet tunas and succulent nopales are the best.

It is the site where the white-winged doves nest.

It is a mystery how the nopales can sometimes glow,

Revealing questions and answers that I should know.

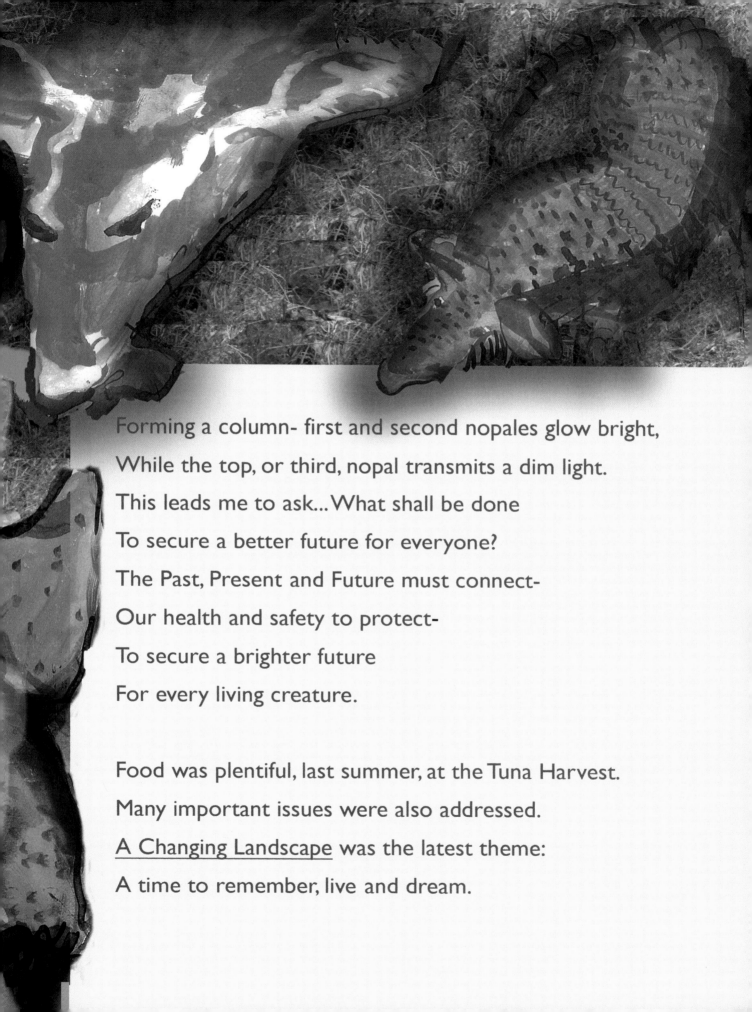

Forming a column- first and second nopales glow bright,

While the top, or third, nopal transmits a dim light.

This leads me to ask... What shall be done

To secure a better future for everyone?

The Past, Present and Future must connect-

Our health and safety to protect-

To secure a brighter future

For every living creature.

Food was plentiful, last summer, at the Tuna Harvest.

Many important issues were also addressed.

A Changing Landscape was the latest theme:

A time to remember, live and dream.

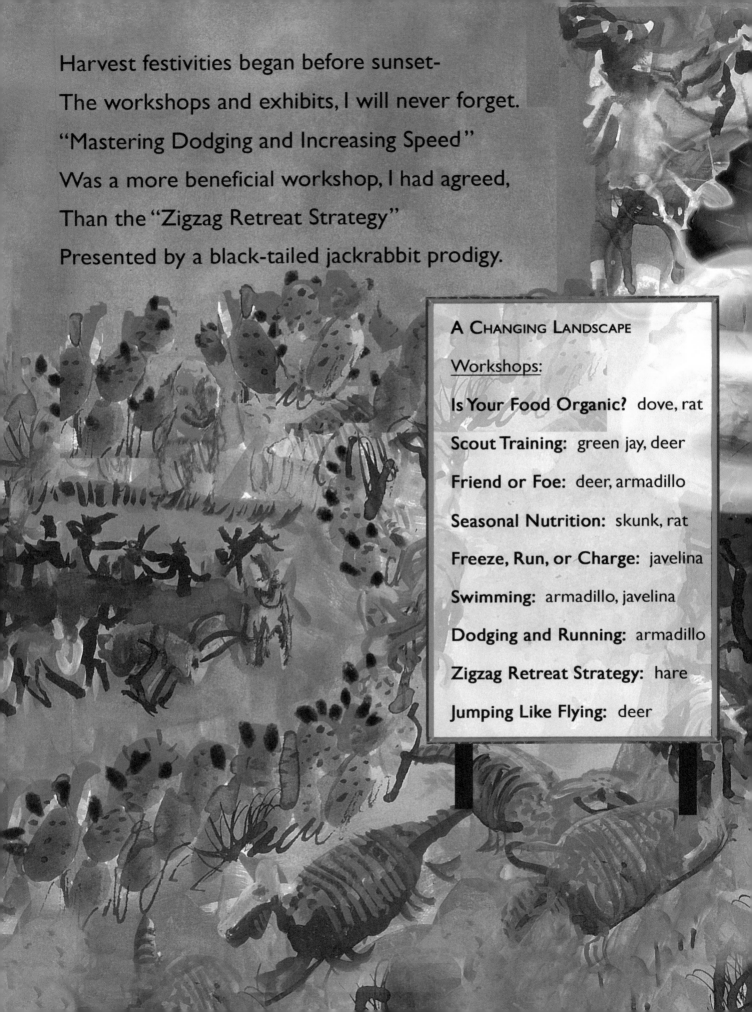

Harvest festivities began before sunset-
The workshops and exhibits, I will never forget.
"Mastering Dodging and Increasing Speed"
Was a more beneficial workshop, I had agreed,
Than the "Zigzag Retreat Strategy"
Presented by a black-tailed jackrabbit prodigy.

A CHANGING LANDSCAPE

Workshops:

Is Your Food Organic? dove, rat

Scout Training: green jay, deer

Friend or Foe: deer, armadillo

Seasonal Nutrition: skunk, rat

Freeze, Run, or Charge: javelina

Swimming: armadillo, javelina

Dodging and Running: armadillo

Zigzag Retreat Strategy: hare

Jumping Like Flying: deer

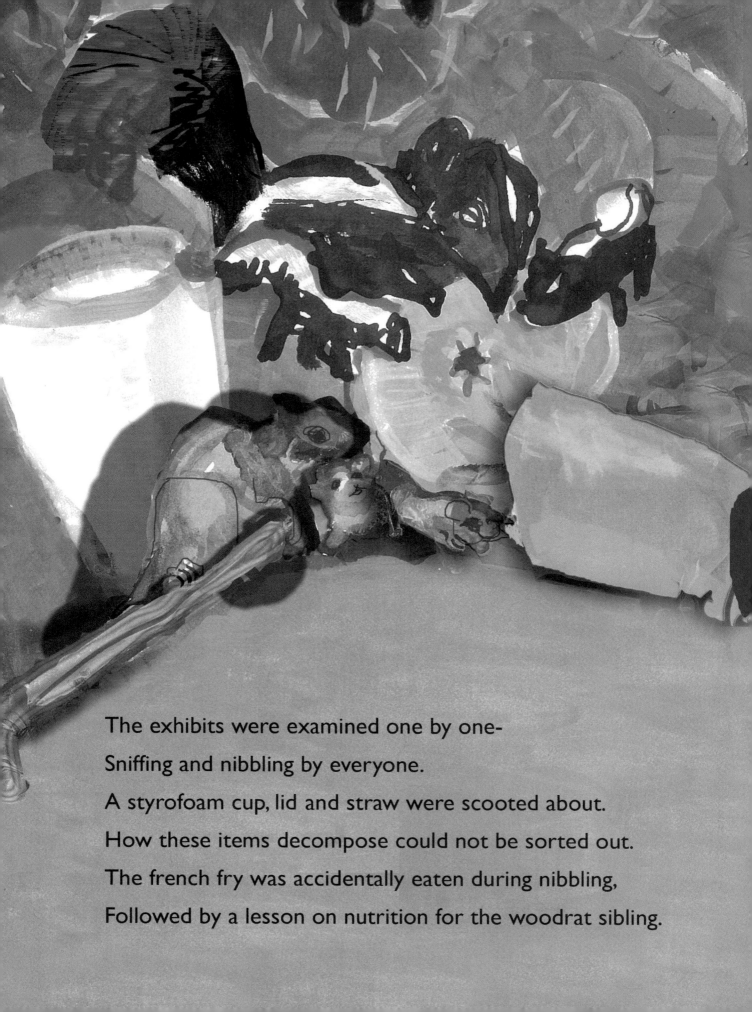

The exhibits were examined one by one-
Sniffing and nibbling by everyone.
A styrofoam cup, lid and straw were scooted about.
How these items decompose could not be sorted out.
The french fry was accidentally eaten during nibbling,
Followed by a lesson on nutrition for the woodrat sibling.

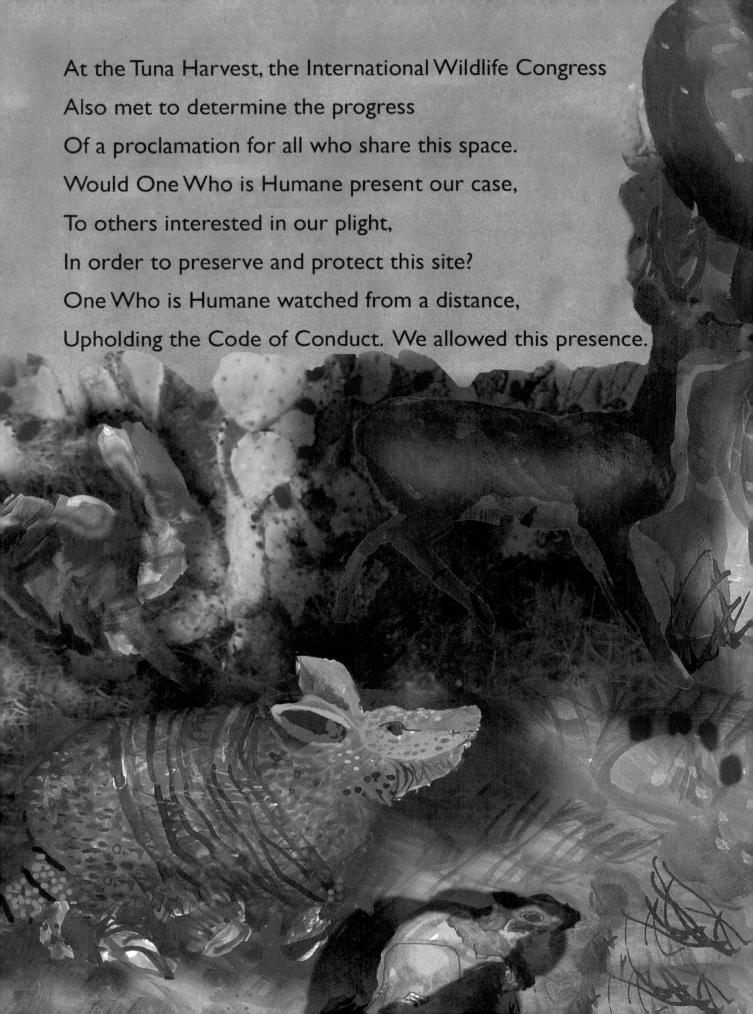

At the Tuna Harvest, the International Wildlife Congress

Also met to determine the progress

Of a proclamation for all who share this space.

Would One Who is Humane present our case,

To others interested in our plight,

In order to preserve and protect this site?

One Who is Humane watched from a distance,

Upholding the Code of Conduct. We allowed this presence.

SANCTUARY CODE OF CONDUCT

Observe wildlife at a distance

Please dim your lights

Dispose of waste properly

Weapons are prohibited

Beware of animal crossings

Conserve natural resources

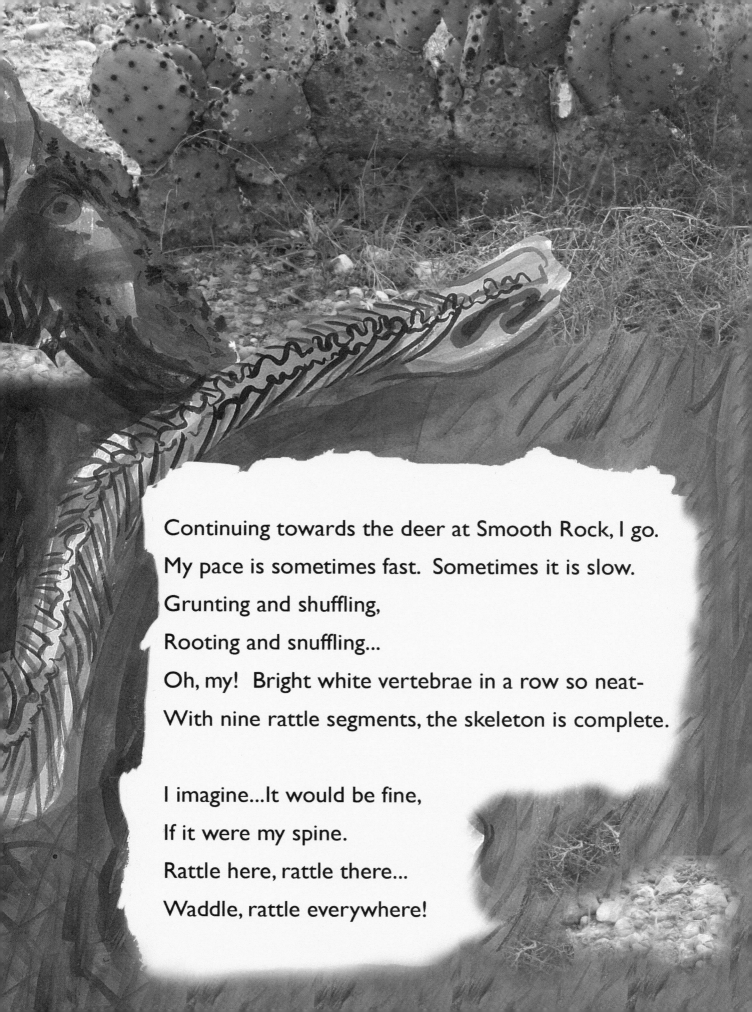

Continuing towards the deer at Smooth Rock, I go.

My pace is sometimes fast. Sometimes it is slow.

Grunting and shuffling,

Rooting and snuffling...

Oh, my! Bright white vertebrae in a row so neat-

With nine rattle segments, the skeleton is complete.

I imagine...It would be fine,

If it were my spine.

Rattle here, rattle there...

Waddle, rattle everywhere!

Suddenly, I hear loud purring and scraping against the ground.
Standing tall and sniffing the air, I slowly turn around.

Hackles erect, the javelina grumbles, "Who is there?"

Huge tusks gleaming- he is a formidable sight and I try not to stare.
"I am looking for my friend, One Who is Humane," I finally say.
"I like your squadron's perfume, by the way."

Sensing no harm, the javelina grunts, "Our friend is not here."

I say, "Then I shall depart, as soon the stars will appear."
I imagine...With razor-sharp tusks such as his,
I could slash through troublesome roots in a whiz!

Interrupting this fantasy,

Of having huge, gleaming tusks such as he,

Is a loud cacophony of multi-lingual cries,

Beneath the hawk that soars in the orange and purple skies.

Running and digging, I quickly respond to this alert-

Pressing my vulnerable belly into the dirt!

Danger having subsided, I resume my journey in the tall grass.

Coming upon a deer's antlers of extraordinary mass,

Which path shall I take? Main beams curve forward,

While sharp points fall downward or rise upward.

Is this the path I am making,

Or are these alternate paths I could be taking?

I imagine...What would it be like if I were wearing these?

If they were my size, I could wear them with ease!

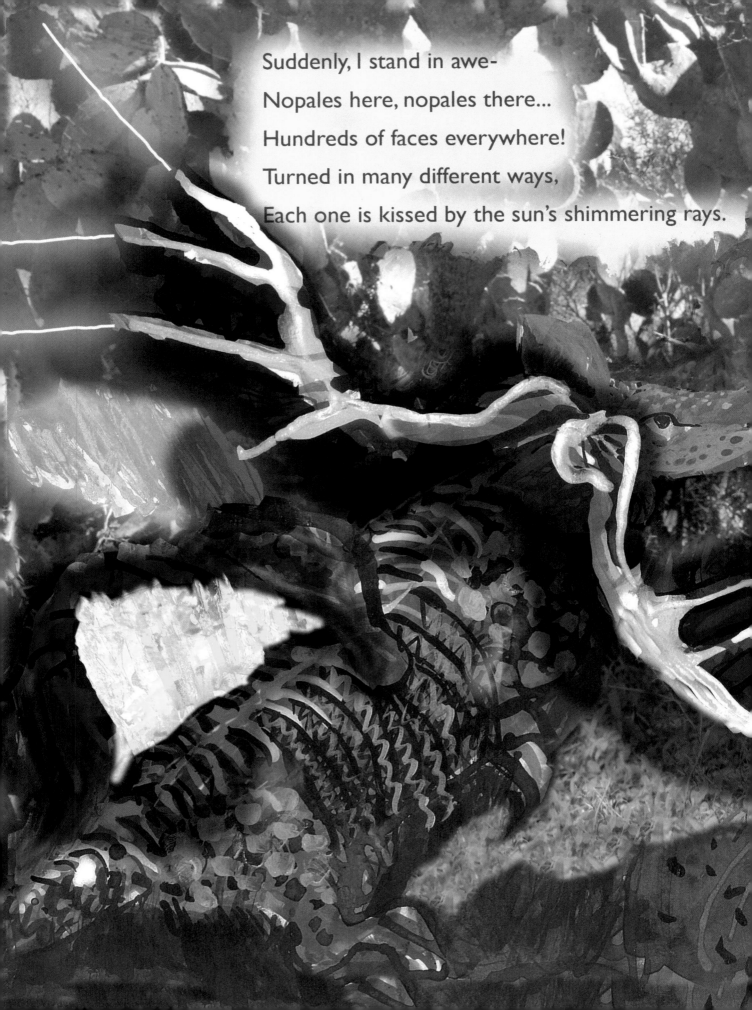

Suddenly, I stand in awe-
Nopales here, nopales there...
Hundreds of faces everywhere!
Turned in many different ways,
Each one is kissed by the sun's shimmering rays.

Shall I go over, around or through the sprawling spiny spaces?

Realistically, flying over the thicket is not among my choices.

I could go around it;

But that would take too long, I admit.

If through the middle is the shortest way,

Then I must put wings, spine, tusks and antlers away.

The three nopales now resemble a towering totem pole-
Standing tall and straight as though on patrol!
My full-bodied armor is just what I need for this prickly passage.
Even the bony rings on my tail work to my advantage.

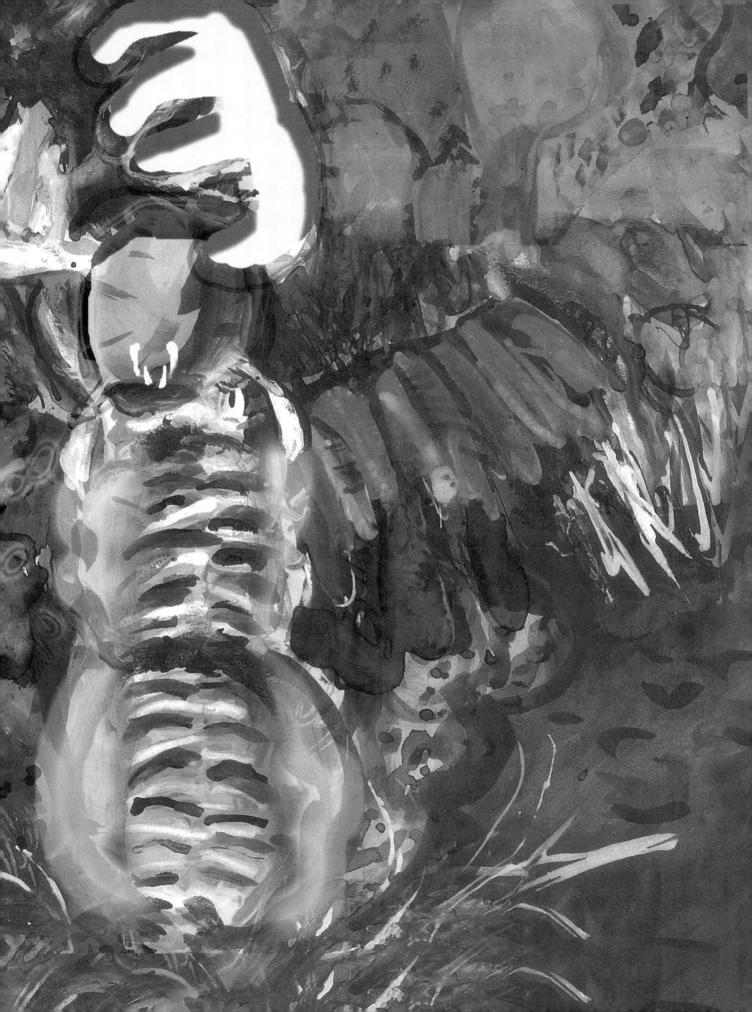

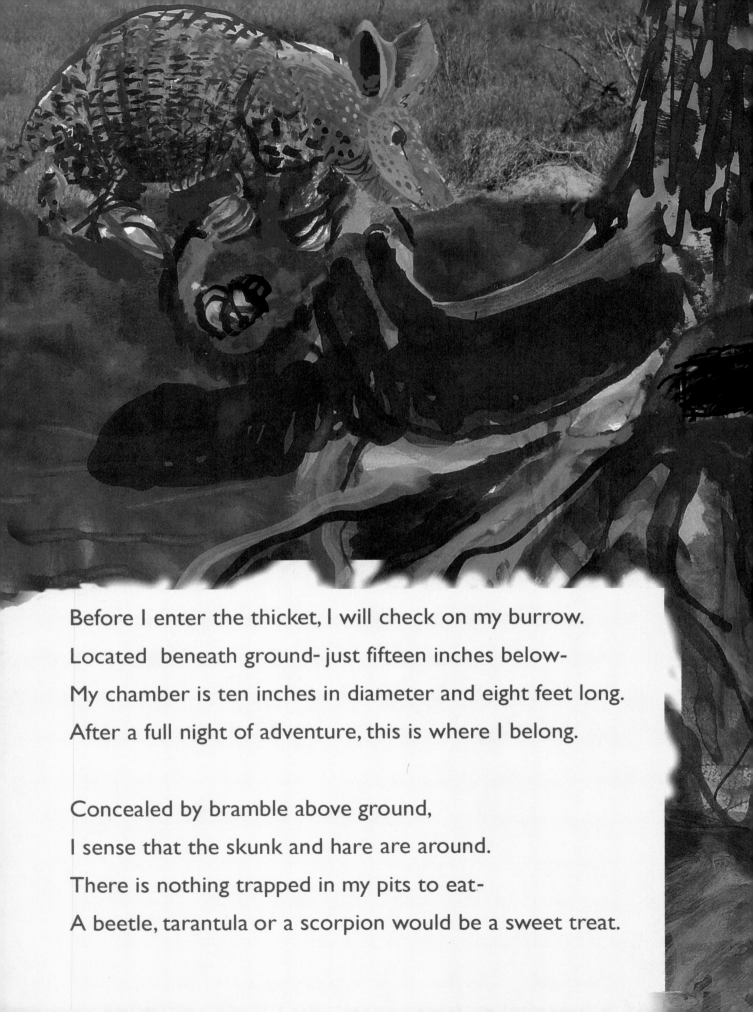

Before I enter the thicket, I will check on my burrow.

Located beneath ground- just fifteen inches below-

My chamber is ten inches in diameter and eight feet long.

After a full night of adventure, this is where I belong.

Concealed by bramble above ground,

I sense that the skunk and hare are around.

There is nothing trapped in my pits to eat-

A beetle, tarantula or a scorpion would be a sweet treat.

Grunting and rooting,

Sniffling and snorting...

Suddenly, I leap.

I smell a grub six inches deep!

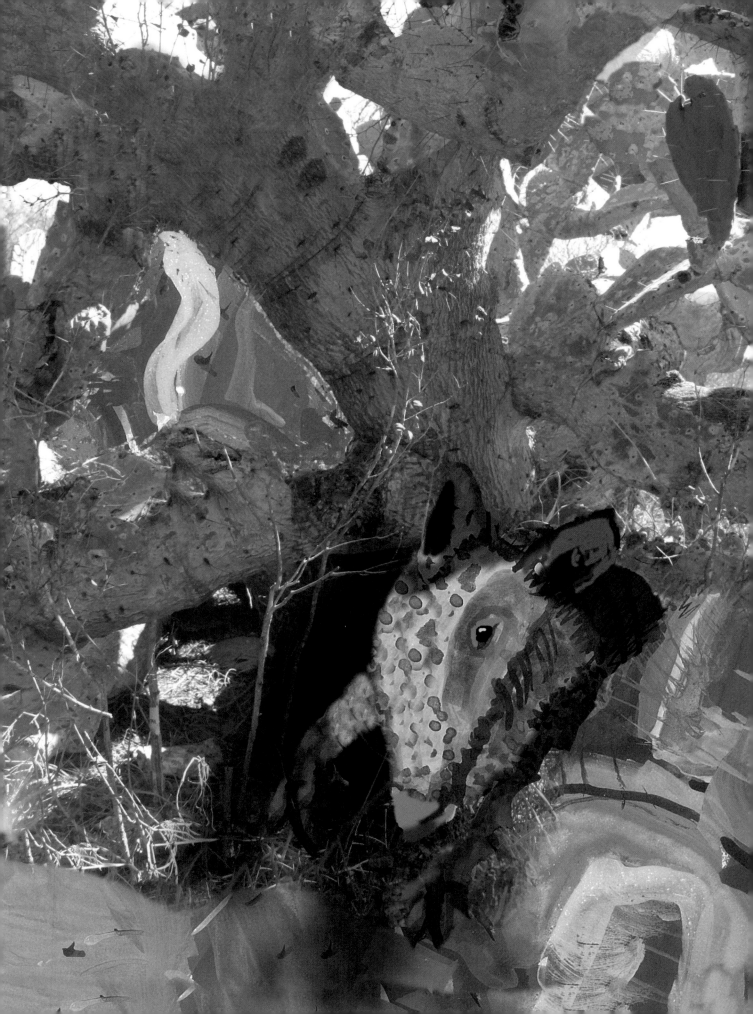

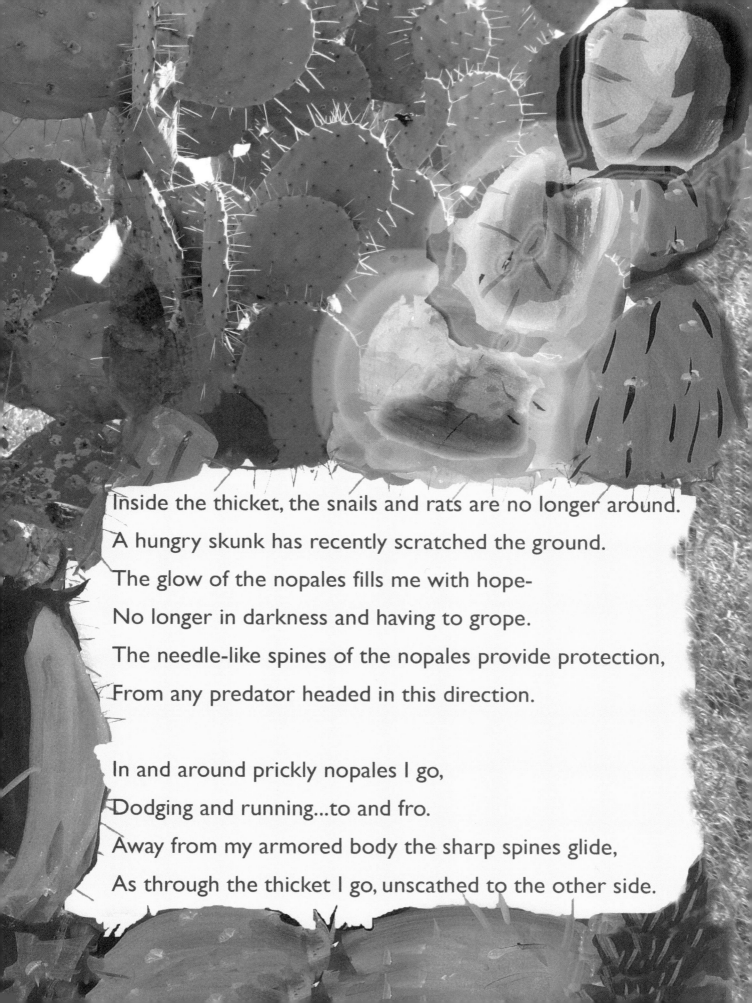

Inside the thicket, the snails and rats are no longer around.

A hungry skunk has recently scratched the ground.

The glow of the nopales fills me with hope-

No longer in darkness and having to grope.

The needle-like spines of the nopales provide protection,

From any predator headed in this direction.

In and around prickly nopales I go,

Dodging and running...to and fro.

Away from my armored body the sharp spines glide,

As through the thicket I go, unscathed to the other side.

To three deer that lay relaxing behind Smooth Rock, I say,

"How are you today?"

Chewing cud in unison, the does sighed

And say, "We are waiting for the traffic to subside."

Across the street, I see that four others are waiting.

"Have you seen One Who is Humane?" I ask without hesitating.

The eldest doe says, "Go to the watering hole at sundown, today.

This is also the night when the pipe organ will play."

Suddenly, they all rise with a gleam in their eyes.

Tall ears and spiked tails- twelve hooves meet ground and skies.

I pause reverently, for we shall soon meet our fate.

I imagine...Can we change the future? Is it ever too late?

Bob Bullock LP

Arriving at our destiny, the watering hole is a site to behold!

We observe from a distance- our Code of Conduct to uphold.

One Who is Humane shines a beam of light,

Revealing an inscription dedicated by others who share our plight.

PROCLAMATION

From this time forth,

We hereby decree:

This land is now and shall forever be

A living sanctuary,

Where animals and humans

Shall live in peace and harmony.

"There are plans to make

And work to undertake,"

One Who is Humane says aloud,

Addressing the small crowd.

"Habitat improvement and restoration

Will benefit all who share spaces at this location."

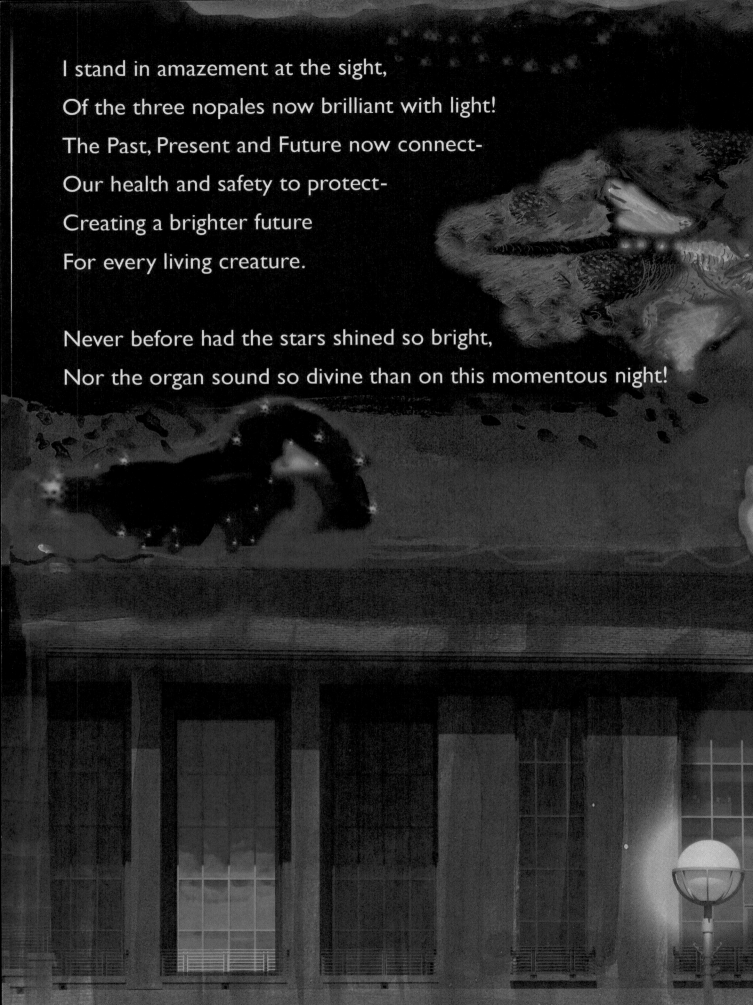

I stand in amazement at the sight,

Of the three nopales now brilliant with light!

The Past, Present and Future now connect-

Our health and safety to protect-

Creating a brighter future

For every living creature.

Never before had the stars shined so bright,

Nor the organ sound so divine than on this momentous night!

CPSIA information can be obtained
at www.ICGtesting.com
Printed in the USA
264509LV00006B

9 781452 009629